MESSY

Also by BARBARA BOTTNER

JUNGLE DAY
or, How I Learned to Love
My Nosey Little Brother

MESSY

Written and illustrated by BARBARA BOTTNER

Delacorte Press/New York

for Rita
who is neat

Published by
Delacorte Press
1 Dag Hammarskjold Plaza
New York, N.Y. 10017

Manufactured in the United States of America

First Printing

Library of Congress Cataloging in Publication Data

Bottner, Barbara.
Messy.

SUMMARY: A six-year-old girl has difficult time
being neat.
[1. Cleanliness—Fiction] I. Title.
PZ7.B6586Me   [E]   78-50420
ISBN 0-440-05492-3
ISBN 0-440-05493-1 lib. bdg.

020946

My real name is Harriet,
but I like to be called Harry.
My mom is always saying,
"Harry, you must be the messiest child
in this town."

I can't help it. My hair is messy even right after I brush it.

My clothes are always messy.

When Mom looks in my room,
she says I must be friends
with a cyclone.

But being messy is the only way
I can find anything.
I keep my leotard and dancing tights
in my hippopotamus book
because the story is about a hippo
who loves to dance.

I know exactly where my favorite toys are:
under my bed. I play there so that Mom won't
make me clean up my room. But she always
finds me and says, "Harry,
how did everything get so messy?"

I don't know.
It's not just because I'm six.
Grace is six and she is neat.
But when she comes over to my house,
she knows we'll have a great time.
At my house we play...

If Mom and I bake a cake,
she lets me mix the icing.
After she cleans up, she says,
"Harry, I think you're trying
to teach me to be messy instead of
me teaching you to be neat."

"Weren't you messy
when you were
a little girl?"
I ask her.

"No, dear.
I was neat."

All the girls in my dance class look like ballerinas.

But I'm the best dancer.
Mrs. Markova says,
"Look at the elevation on Harriet."
That means I jump high.

I can twirl
the longest

and bend the farthest.

One day Mrs. Markova says,
"We're going to have a recital.
I'm going to give out costumes
and I hope everyone takes good care of them.
Harry, I want you to be the princess."

Then she gives me a white tutu
with the most ruffles
I've ever seen.
It's fluffy, like a white cloud.
I don't want it to get rumpled
because then I won't look
like a real princess.

When I get home, I show Mom my costume.
"I'm going to be neat, Mom, just like a princess."
"Oh, Harry, that's wonderful," she says.

I spend all week washing my stuffed animals, fixing my drawers,
finding the pieces to my puzzles,
and putting away all my loose crayons.
"I'm really trying," I tell Mom.
"I know," she answers.

On the day of the recital
Mom takes out the white tutu.
It still looks like a white cloud.
She ties a ribbon in my hair
and gives me a big hug.

I'm not nervous because I know I'm the best in my class.
When the curtain opens, I twirl around and around without stopping.
But Grace falls down and Mrs. Markova has to pull her off the stage.

At the end everyone claps.
They clap very loud for me.
Dad gives me roses
and I feel like a real princess.

Mom takes my picture and says,
"Today you don't look messy at all."

"But Mom, I've been neat
for a whole week!"

Then we go to a restaurant for dessert.
Mom says I can order anything I want.
I get hot pecan pie with chocolate-chip ice cream
and coconut fudge cream on top.

Just as I'm twirling my napkin
like a flying bird,
Dad reaches over to get the cream.

ABOUT THE AUTHOR / ARTIST

Barbara Bottner has been an elementary school teacher, an actress, a book reviewer, and an award-winning film-maker and illustrator. She has written and illustrated several picture books, including JUNGLE DAY OR, HOW I LEARNED TO LOVE MY NOSEY LITTLE BROTHER.

ABOUT THE BOOK

The art for this book was prepared on Strathmore paper with Negro lead pencils. Overlays were done on vellum with stubs. The art for the cover was drawn in pen and pencil and colored inks. The text has been set on Alphatype in Tiffany Light with Demi by Boro Typographers, Inc. The book was printed by General Offset and bound by Economy Bookbinding Corp.